Hi! I'm KT.
My parents are
divorced.

Sam and I
live with my mom.

Meow

Who do you live with?

1

Please draw a picture of you and the grown-up you live with.

Art by
2 **Peter Winter**

BOULDEN PUBLISHING
P.O.Box 1186, Weaverville, CA 96093
Phone (800) 238-8433

Editor
Evelyn Mercer Ward

Sometimes I feel sad and lonely
because I miss my Dad.

It is okay for me to feel mad or glad
or any other way.

How do you feel about living with one parent?

Mom and I share the housework.
We are a team.

	MON	TUES	WED	THUR	FRI
DISHES	KT	MOM	KT	MOM	
	M	KT	M	KT	M
SET TABLE	KT	M	KT	M	KT	M
GARB.	M	KT	M	KT	M	
PICK UP	KT	M	KT	M	KT

We have agreed on a list of jobs for Mom and me.

I hate cleaning the cat litter box, so Mom and I take turns doing that.

KittyBox

What do you do to help out around the house?

Mom and I have good times together.

We both like to play games and
go to the beach.

What are some fun things you like to do with your parent?

Mom always tells me where she is going
and when she will be back.

She leaves a phone number
where I can call her.

I keep the door locked and don't
let anyone in.

Are you ever alone at home? How does that feel?

Draw a picture of you at home alone.

I hate it when Mom brings home a date. Sometimes they forget about me.

Mom says she needs grown-up friends. Her love for me is different.

How do you feel when your mom or dad dates?

Mom sometimes asks me what she should do about her grown-up problems.

I tell her that I don't know.
I am just a kid.

How do you feel when a grown-up tells you their problems?

When I am mad at Mom, I sometimes call my dad.

Dad tells me to work it out with my mom

This gets everyone upset.

Why is it a bad idea to tell one parent about all your problems with the other parent?

It makes me sad when my mom and dad say mean things about each other.

I don't want to be in their fights.
I love them both.

How do you feel when your mom and dad talk mean to each other?

Mom often gets very tired because she has to do the work of two parents.

I wish she didn't have to work so much. It helps if I let her rest.

What can you do to help your mom or dad more?

Mom sometimes says mean things to me when she is tired.

It is best for me to leave her alone until she feels better.

What do you do when your mom or dad is in a bad mood?

Mom and I go through both good times and bad times together.

We take care of each other.

What are some things your mom or dad has done for you?

It helps when Mom and I talk about our feelings.

We are lucky to have each other.

What would you like to tell your mom or dad?

Content Editors

We are grateful to the many professionals who contributed their time and experience in the development of this publication.
Special recognition is extended to the following counselors:
Christy Reinold, Una Simental, Shelly Borchardt, Joanna Hansen, Nancy Prisk, Cherri Stefanic and Nancy Motter.

My
Very Best
Rainy Day!

Written and illustrated by

P.K. Hallinan

Ideals Children's Books • Nashville, Tennessee

Published by Ideals Publishing Corporation
Nashville, Tennessee 37210

Printed and bound in the United States of America.

ISBN 0-8249-8497-8

It's a wonderful
nothing-to-do rainy day!
The rain's falling gently.
The world's a soft gray.

Just grab your umbrella
and be on your way.
It's a wonderful
nothing-to-do rainy day!

4

It's time to go splashing
on rain-covered lawns.

5

And time to go dashing
through puddles and ponds.

It's time for launching
a fabulous fleet
of walnut-shell sailboats
to sail past your feet.

When there's nothing to do
there's really no end
to the things you can think of,
or dream, or pretend.

You can work, if you like,
on fixing your bike.

You can mend the old dent
where your tow truck is bent.

You can even start building
a playhouse for two,
with a trapdoor so small
only you can crawl through.

You can bake a mud pie.

You can watch worms go by.

You can zoom all around
like a jet in the sky.

It's all up to you
what you do or you play
on this wonderful
nothing-to-do rainy day!

15

But maybe you'd rather
just stay warm and dry
and make up some games
that take you inside.

Like trying each crayon
on your coloring books . . .

or painting your face
just to see how it looks.

18

Or maybe it's time
to go up to your room
and set up a tent
with a bedspread and broom.

And then you can howl
like a great, hooting owl.

Then much later on,
about quarter to three,
there's nothing like popcorn
and a little TV.

20

Yes, you'll find that the grayest
of days can be bright
if you treat them like presents
from morning till night.

21

So don't ever worry
when the clouds start to form.
Just think of the wonders
that come with each storm . . .

A hot cup of cocoa,
a warm, cheery blaze . . .

23

and wonderful
nothing-to-do rainy days!